HOW-TO COWBOY

22 SECRET, MAGIC HOW-TO FUN TRICKS

To Maddie

Written by

Edward Allan Faine

Illustrated by

Joan C. Waites

Happy Highways!

IM Press

Third Printing 2010
Manufactured in the United States of America

IM Press
P.O. Box 5346
Takoma Park, Maryland 20913-5346
301-587-1202
efaine@yahoo.com

Visit www.howtocowboy.com

Other books by Edward Allan Faine last four pages

and

www.google.com/profiles/edwardallanfaine

Children events by Edward Allan Faine last page

CONTENTS

HOW TO

HOW TO TALK LIKE DONALD DUCK

1) First try a warmup. Place tongue near roof of mouth. Blow gently. Tongue will flap. Sound high note in throat. Continue to blow. Press tongue tightly to roof of mouth.

2) Presto! You've got a police whistle. Start. Stop. Breeet! Breeet!

3) Now for the Donald. With mouth open, place tongue to the right side of mouth and blow hard. Tongue will vibrate. Skew mouth to left.

4) Blow HARD. Really HARD. Tongue and cheek will vibrate wildly. You'll sound like a humped-back, crazed tabby cat, hair on end, fending off a doberman pinsher.

5) Practice alone, away from others so as to not embarrass yourself or frighten your family.

6) Now you are ready to do Donald Duck. Repeat 4) above, keeping tongue and mouth skewed to the right, but blow moderately.

7) Mouth words. Say "Hello, I Love You, Shutup." Say anything.

8) Don't worry if you don't sound like Donald right away. Along as you're squawking and honking, you'll be okay. Think of a goose if it helps.

9) Practice. Talk loud. Talk soft. Change shape of mouth while talking. Listen to yourself. In time you'll get it.

10) Read Donald Duck comic books. Watch Donald Duck videos. Sleep on Donald Duck sheets. Take a trip to DisneyLand or Disney World.

11) To imitate the upset (flustered) Donald, vigourously shake head back and forth while making the basic sound. Feel both cheeks flap.

12) Greet friends and strangers alike in your new Donald voice. People will smile. You'll be popular.

A man walks into a psychiatrist's office with a duck on a leash. "Doctor, Doctor, my brother's crazy, he thinks he's a duck."

The doctor replies, "So, why don't you take him down to the pond and set him free."

The man hangs his head and sighs. "I would, but he's the cartoon voice of Donald Duck, and we need the money."

Skew mouth to left

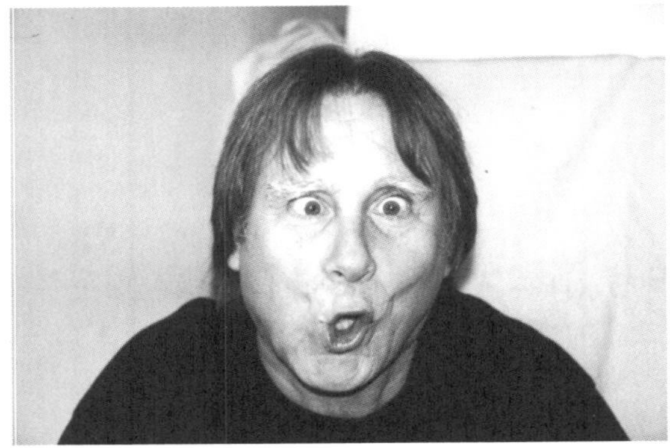

Don't stick tongue in right cheek

HOW TO BAFFLE YOUR FRIENDS (Rule of Three)

1) Do you believe in three? You will after you baffle your friends with these three tricks.

2) Write "You Chose Three" on a strip of paper. Fold it up.

3) Tell your friend to hold the folded paper in their right hand, but don't look at it.

4) Ask your pal, "Choose a number, one , two or three." Quickly add, "But don't tell me, just nod when you've picked the number."

5) Say, "Now, look at the paper." Watch her mouth drop. She'll ask, "How'd you know". Tell her, "I'm a clairvoyant." (Tell her to look up the word in the dictionary).

6) Approach another friend. Hand him the same folded strip of paper.

7) Show him another piece of paper with the numbers one, two, three and four written on it.

8) Ask him to circle one of the four numbers.

9) Say, "Now look at the folded paper." His eyes will pop, and he'll shake his head in disbelief, and ask if you are clairvoyant. You nod.

10) Shove three grapes, checkers, marbles, whatevers, in front of another buddy. Number the objects one, two, three. Hand him the folded paper as before, then say, "Pick one."

11) Ask him to read the folded paper. Watch his left eyebrow arch.

12) Beware of those who pick a number other than three. Keep your eyes on them.

"...whether it's the classic fable or fairy tale or folktale, or a B-movie on television—you'll notice that the number three holds strong sway. Character triangles make the stongest character combinations and are the most common in stories. Events also tend to happen in threes. The hero tries three times to overcome an obstacle. He fails the first two times and succeeds the third."
20 MASTER PLOTS by Ronald B. Tobias (1993)

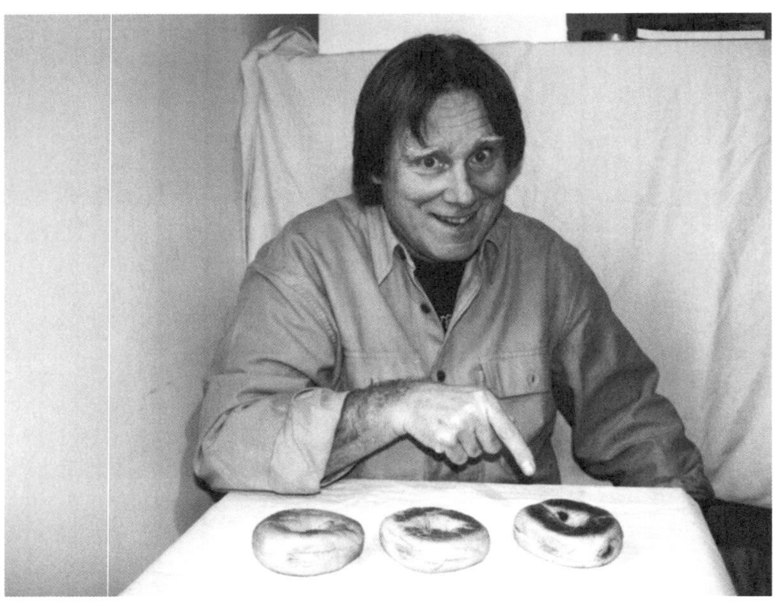

HOW TO NAME YOUR ROCK BAND

1) What was your first pet's name? Example: Squeaky

2) What was the name of the first street you lived on? Example: Fry

3) You got it! Squeaky Fry! Backwards works sometimes, too.

4) Imagine the radio annnoucer: "Put your hands together and give it up for that new international sensation, Squeaky Fry.

5) Now you need to name your first song. What's your favorite color? Example: Red.

6) What's your favorite food? Example: French Fries.

7) Announcer: "For the tenth straight week, the undisputed number one song in America, Red French Fries by Squeaky Fry. Yaaaaaaaaay!

8) Good. But now you need a name for the lead singer.

9) What was the name of the first movie you ever saw? Example: Bambi.

10) What is your favoriite toothpaste? Mouthwash? Example: Colgate. Scope.

11) Announcer: "Here she is, America's newest songbird, Bambi Scope and her band Squeaky Fry!"

12) Now to name the first album, the first CD.

13) What is your favorite fruit? Favorite vegetable? Example: Banana. String Beans.

14) Jay Leno: "And now, fresh from their first European tour, playing their hit, Red French Fries, from their platinum CD, Banana String Beans, it's Bambi Scope and her band Squ-eeeea-kky Fryyyyyy!

"If it wasn't for Alan Freed, rock 'n' roll might have gone by another name. After joining Cleveland radio station WJW in 1951, DJ Alan Freed began introducing black R&B music to white teenage audiences on his weekly Moondog Rock 'n' Roll Party." Rock and Roll Museum, Cleveland, Ohio

How-To Cowboy playing "air drums"

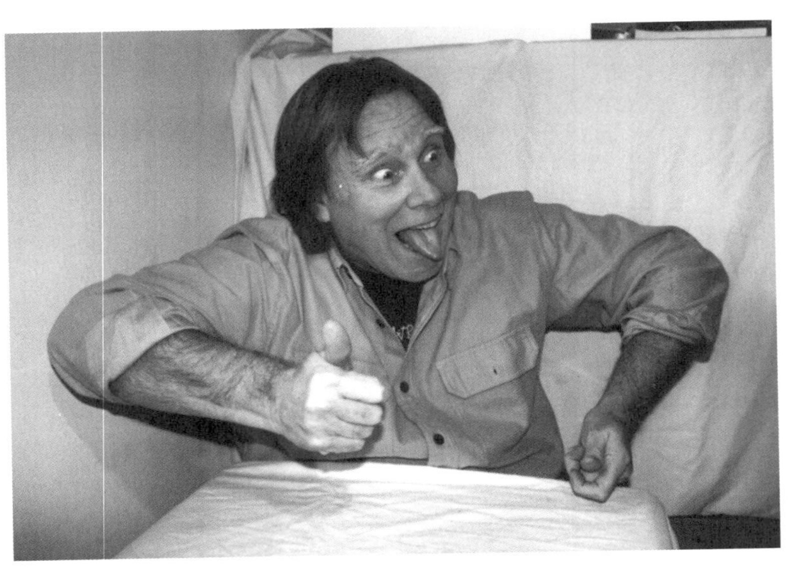

HOW TO PLAY HAND TRUMPET

1) Cup hands as if to hold a buzzing firefly.

2) Left hand on top, right hand wrapped around back.

3) Thumbs up, pressed together, gently.

4) Blow down in thumb hole. Softly, then hard. Ah! sound! And on the first try, too!

5) Narrow hand cup. Blow a high note.

6) Widen hand cup. Blow a low note.

7) Stick right hand out. Blow hard. Hit high note.

8) Vary right right hand position, out halfway, say. Blow soothing mellow tone.

9) Note that air volume and embrochure affect pitch. Practice making different sounds.

10) Use tongue to articulate, blow smart clipped notes.

11) Flutter tongue to make a police whistle sound.

12) Hum while blowing to play a chord.

13) Put it all together. Play a tune.
Play, "Yes Sir, she's my baby." Or how about Prokofiev's "March of the Three Oranges?"

14) Practice every day. On the way home from school. In your room. Don't bug your parents.

15) When ready, form a band (drums, bass, piano or guitar), book gigs at local venues. Play dances, weddings. Become famous.

When trumpet legend Louis 'Satchmo' Armstrong was asked if jazz was folk music, Armstrong replied, "Man, all music is folk music. You ain't never heard no horse sing a song, have you?"

To make a hand trumpet: Raise your left arm like you are going to do a karate chop. Curve the left hand, and then bring the right hand over to the left — as if to shake hands — making sure the thumbs touch, as shown below:

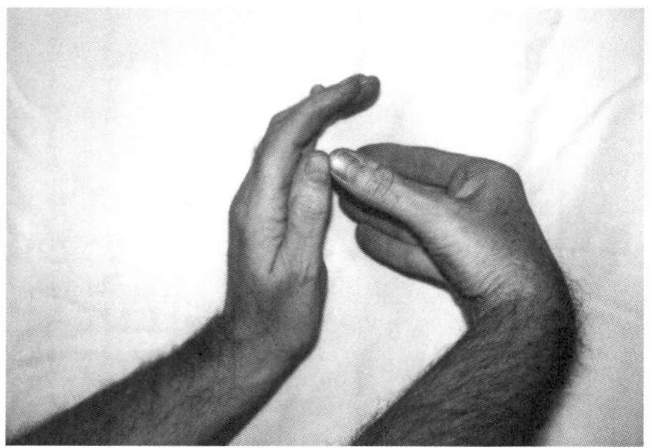

Lay the left hand fingers on top of the right hand. Close the "back door," wrap right hand fingers around the back as shown below. The next step is to bring the bottoms of your thumbs together and you have formed a hand trumpet as shown in the cover illustration.

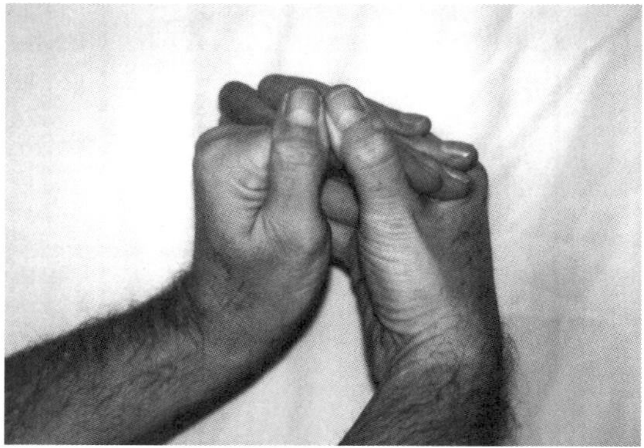

HOW TO
DUPE DOPES
(Order of Siam)

1) Form a secret club with friends. Name it the Royal Order of SIAM.

2) Nominate leaders, give them fancy names: Potentate, Grand Wizar, Prince of Records.

3) Draw up bylaws, charter. Make them mysterious, esoteric, secretive. Be creative.

4) Recruit new members (dopes).

5) Invite them to a midnight initiation ceremony around a bonfire.

6) Members wear fancy costumes, talk in mysterious code.

7) Speak of the ancient lineage of
the Order, the need for secrecy and daily ritualistic homage to the diety TAGU.

8) Now comes the fun part. The potentate commands dopes to face bonfire, kneel, bow heads, place their outstretched arms on the ground.

9) He next orders them to raise up, arms oustretched, reaching skyward.

10) Dopes repeat exercize, down, up, down, up, and begin to slowly chant homage to the almighty TAGU, ruler of SIAM: "AHWA-TAGU-SIAM."

11) Potentate orders recruits to repeat bowing and chanting. Again, but faster.

12) Faster. "AHWA-TAGU-SIAM." And faster.

13) Dopes will come to their senses, realize what they are chanting. "Oh, what a goose I am." Be nice to dopes afterward. No one likes being duped, even though it's instructive.

“Hello, sucker!”
Texas (Mary Louise Cecilia) Guinan (1884-1933)

“There is a sucker born every minute.”
Phineas Taylor Barnum (1810-1891)

“Never give a sucker an even break”
Edward Francis Albee (1857-1930)

HOW TO MAKE MUSICAL MILK

1) Sit at wooden table. Make double, double sure the table is made of wood.

2) Find a metal fork, one with flexible prongs, like Grandma's fork.

3) Pluck the middle prongs so they make a "ting" sound. Hold in left hand, pluck with right hand (reverse if left-handed). Hold fork in air, do not rest on table.

4) Make the "ting" sound several times. Practice. Get good at it.

5) Now, pluck the fork prongs, "ting", then gently place the fork on the wooden table. Listen to the resonant "wow wow wow" echo sound. Practice this several times.

6) Now the fun part. Find a glass. Fill it with milk. Place it on the wood table. Find a friend (sucker).

7) Tell the sucker you are going to make musical milk, make milk sing.

8) Tell the sucker you are going to take the fork's "ting" sound, place it in the milk glass, and the milk will respond with a ringing "wow wow wow" sound like the fat lady at the opera.

9) Do it. But DON'T let the sucker see you put the fork on the table.

10) Watch the sucker's mouth drop.

11) Do it again, with flare. The sucker will say, "Oooh, aaah. How did you do that?" Don't tell.

12) Now you know how to make musical milk. Book yourself on television. Become a star. But don't get a swell head.

"Cow Cow Boogie" an early boogie woogie tune was penned (appropriately) by Chicago vaudevillian Charles "Cow Cow" Davenport (circa 1923).

HOW TO TEACH A CAT TO ROLL OVER

1) Befriend a nice cat.

2) Give it good scritchies everyday. Scritch the neck and belly while on its side or back.

3) Mimic the cat's voice (meow, whine, gurgle) while scritching.

4) Do this everyday for a month.

5) Train the cat to expect a healthy round of scritchies after you call to it in its meow or purr gurgly voice.

6) This is the first step in teaching a cat to rollover on command.

7) If you follow this regimen for a month, the cat will come to you when you call, flop at your feet, on its back, ready for scritchies. Cats are pretty smart, you know.

8) Now comes the second step. Call the cat. Don't give scritchies. Instead, point your finger to the left (cat's eye level), move it to the right. In time, the cat will follow finger and eventually roll to the right.

9) Reward the cat with generous scritchies every time the cat rolls.

10) Next step. The rollover.
Repeat steps 8-9, but this time,
make a left to right (clockwise) circle.

11) Cat will eventually understand and rollover completely. Reward with a double dose of super scritchies.

12) Call your friends, show them your trick. They'll be wowed! Be humble. Reward cat.

"Nice" Midnight the Cat to Smilin' Ed McConnell every Saturday morning on Smilin' Ed's Buster Brown Gang radio show on CBS (1944-1952).

Angus and Phoebe in training for the World's First Cat Roll Over Competition to be held in Catmandu, Nepal in the summer of 2004.

HOW TO MAKE SURREAL CEREAL

1) Shake cornflakes into a bowl.

2) Pour in fresh orange juice. Taste. Slurp up. Neat, huh?!

3) Next day, use frozen orange juice with bubbly carbonated water.

4) Repeat steps 1 through 2. Ooo-oooh! Yummy-good!

5) How about wheat flakes? Rice chex? Corn puffs?

6) How about tangerine juice? Grape juice? Cranberry? Kool-Aid? The list is endlesssssssssssssssss.

7) How about marshmallows? Hershey kisses? Pretzels? Oreos? Honey-roasted cashew nuts? Moon-Pie crumbles? Twinkies?
The list is endlesssssssssssssssss.

8) Ladle rolled oats into a bowl.

9) Pour on chocolate milk. Eat. Scree-umptiously groovy.

10) Next day, make hot cocoa with buttermilk.

11) Repeat steps 8 through 10. Lovely. Devine lusciousness.

12) You're on your own. Be creative. Add everything but cooked turnips and oysters.

13) Just think what you could do at a Motel breakfast buffet.

14) People will think you're crazy. Grow thick skin.

"Okay, folks, it's time to march around the breakfast table"   Don McNeill every morning on The Breakfast Club radio show out of Chicago on the NBC network (1933-1968)

"Hey Mikey! He likes it! "   Life cereal TV commercial (1976-1989)

HOW TO HYPNOTIZE A FROG

1) Catch a frog.

2) Wash your hands.

3) Rinse the frog in lukewarm water.

4) Pat dry.

5) Lay the frog on its back, gently.

6) Hold it down with your left pointer finger and thumb (right, if left handed). Place left pointer finger on one frog shoulder, left thumb on the other shoulder.

7) Take right pointer finger and rub the frog's white slippery belly in a circle, round and round.

8) Don't press too hard. Be nice.

9) Count to twenty, softly, slowly.

10) Lift finger.

11) Frog should be hypnotized (totally relaxed). If not, repeat steps 7 through 10.

12) Turn frog over. Snap your fingers. Say "Bree-dup, Bree-dup." Tickle its bottom.

13) Otherwise, be careful what you do and say, frogs are acutely susceptible to the power of suggestion.

14) In five-ten minutes the frog will wake up, hop away.

15) Say goodbye. Wipe your fingers, keep them out of your mouth.

"Plunk your magic twanger, Froggy" Smilin' Ed McConnell to Froggy the Gremlin every Saturday morning on Smilin' Ed's Buster Brown Gang radio show on CBS (1944-1952).

The How-To Cowboy as a very young man about to cast his hypnotic spell on an unsuspecting frog.

Aquatic Gardens, Kensington, Maryland, circa 1970

HOW TO MAKE SOUR SWEET

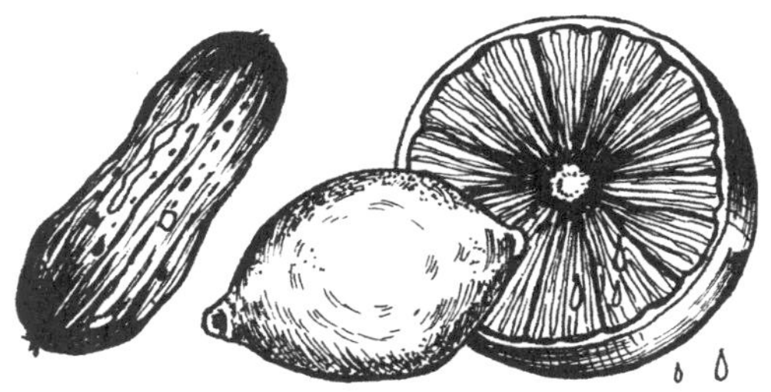

1) Cut a grapefruit in half. Your mouth is watering already, isn't it?

2) Sprinkle on SALT. Not SUGAR!

3) Taste. Sweet, isn't it!

4) Sour things on sour things make them double sweet.

5) Ever bite into a ripe onion? Stingy, sharp and sour, right?

6) Cut that eye-watering burny onion taste with lard! Make a onion-lard sandwich, and pretend you're a depression-era, rail-riding hobo.

7) Spead lard on two slices of thick bread. Pile on the onion slices. Take a bite.

8) Sweet. Heavenly. Ahhhhh!

9) Here's another: works best at holiday family meals or banquets.

10) Lemon pie. Tart, right? Lemon Merenque pie? Just as sour.

11) Pour gravy on the lemon pie. Beef or pork gravy, it doesn't matter.

12) Ummm! The pie's not tangy anymore, sort of marshmallowy.

13) Find a big juicy dill pickle.

14) Dip it in soft vanilla ice cream. Swirl it around. Now bite.

15) Not sour anymore is it? What does it taste like?

16) Life is just a bowl of cherries. Don't get delirious, it's not mysterious.

"Chewing the food of sweet and bitter fancy" As You Like It by William Shakespeare (1564-1616)

The How-To Cowboy enjoys his favorite evening snack. Um, um, yummy, good! A fat, warty, slimy dill pickle and vanilla ice cream. Delicious! (Ice cream is low-fat).

HOW TO WHISTLE THROUGH YOUR TONGUE

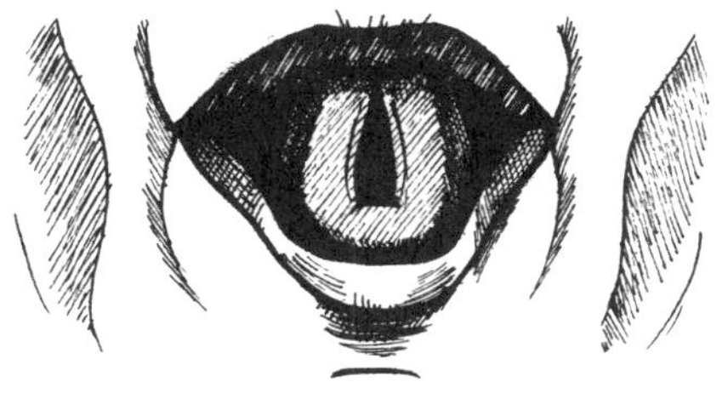

1) Make your mouth juicy, think of a lemon.

2) Lick your lips.

3) Stick your little finger (the pinky) in the center of your mouth up to the first knuckle.

4) Remove pinky, but hold your round mouth hole thus created.

5) Curl your tongue inside your mouth.

6) Poke your tongue through the round mouth hole.

7) Blow gently. Listen for sound.

8) Relax. Repeat steps 1 through 7.

9) Blow gently, blow hard, listen for low notes, high notes.

10) Change shape of tongue hole. Blow. Narrow for high notes, wide for low notes.

11) Stick tongue flute all the way out. Blow. Listen. Pull tongue flute in. Listen again.

12) To trill, shake head.

13) To mute, cup hands over mouth. To play a chord, hum.

14) You are ready for your first song. Try Jingle Bells, Yankee Doodle Dandy. Practice. Think Carnegie Hall.

15) Now you can whistle through your tongue. Impress your friends. Become an important person.

"You know how to whistle don't you, Steve? Just put your lips together... and blow."
Lauren Bacall to Humphrey Bogart in TO HAVE AND HAVE NOT (1944)

Think of your tongue as a musical instrument, a fife or a flute. Note that the the fife is formed with the tongue, yes, but also by the roof of the mouth, and especially the upper lip. Now think of your tongue whistle as a trombone. Slide your tongue in and out while blowing until you get a sound. Too far out, nothing. Too far in, nothing. Find the spot where the tongue just rests on the lower lip, just peeking ouside your puckered lips.

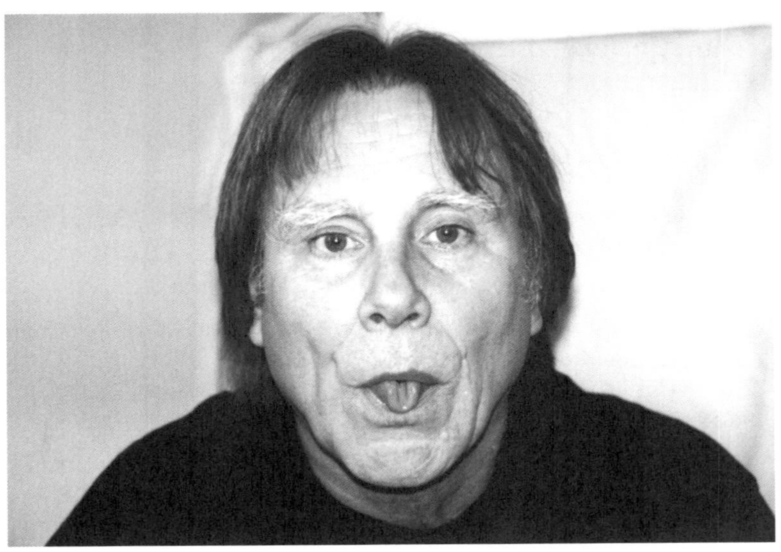

HOW TO ALWAYS WIN AT CHECKERS

1) View the checker board NOT as a jumble of light and dark squares, but as 8 columns criss-crossed by 8 rows (a column is the up and down vertical stack of squares, a row is the side to side horizontal lineup of squares.)

2) Focus on the columns (at the right time) and you'll always win at checkers.

3) Pick a partner (the chump).

4) Begin the game as you always do. Play smart.

5) After you and chump lose 3 checkers apiece, think columns.

6) Before you make a move, note the number of TOTAL checkers (yours and the chumps) in each column.

7) You want to keep an odd number of TOTAL checkers (1, 3, 5) in each column if possible, never an even number (2, 4, 6). (Remember, count your checkers, and the chump's checkers.)

8) So, whenever possible, move your checker <u>from</u> an even checkered column <u>to</u> an even checkered column, leaving behind an odd numbered column, and creating a new odd numbered one. Oh joy!

9) Continue to play smart. Never move your piece into a triple jump, just to make an odd column.

10) The odd column trick gives you (and not the chump) the edge, the last move, the winning move.

11) Use this tip and you'll always win at checkers. Another tip. It always helps to choose a dumb partner.

"It was a little cocker spaniel... black and white spotted. And our little girl Tricia... named it Checkers. And you know, the kids love that dog, and I just want to say this right now, that regardless of what they say about it, we're going to keep it."
- Senator Richard Milhouse Nixon in a TV broadcast to the nation on September 23,1952.

The How-To Cowboy always makes the right move! (See picture below). The Cowboy moves his bottom row checker from the third to the second column, thus creating an odd number of checkers in rows two and three (where before there was an even number). Got it?

HOW TO TIE A NEAT KNOT

1) Find a foot-long 1/8" — 1/4" rope or shoelace.

2) Pretend one end of the rope is a very hungry mouse. Mark it with a crayon or magic marker.

3) Pretend the loop you make in the rope 8" from the mouse, is a mouse hole. Clamp the hole at the bottom with left forefinger and thumb. Grab the mouse with right forefinger and thumb.

4) Now... pretend the mouse pokes its head through the mouse hole ready to make a mad dash for the pantry.

5) The coast is clear. The mouse scampers toward the pantry, BUT THEN... it hears a noise. "Meow!" "It's a cat!" The frightened mouse ducks behind the broom handle (the non-marked rope end) and waits.

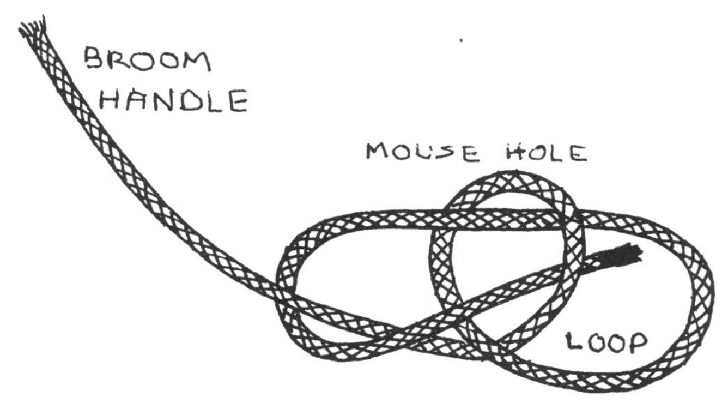

6) Now switch hands. The right thumb and forefinger clamp onto the bottom of the mouse hole, and the left thumb and forefinger hold the mouse. The mouse hears "Me-ow," and runs straight to its mouse hole and jumps through.

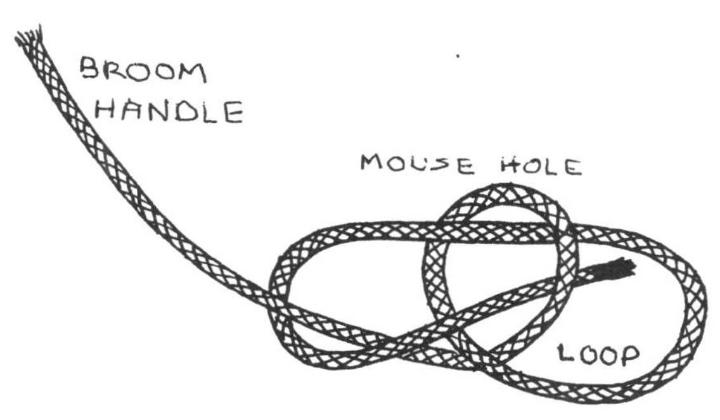

7) Now, grab the broom handle with the left forefinger and thumb, the mouse with the right forefinger and thumb, and pull gently and tightly. Ta Da! You've tied a neat knot!

8) What you've got is a bowline knot, pronounced "bow-lin," the only knot you'll ever need, the most useful knot in all of knottydom.

9) The big loop you've created goes around a tent peg or a piling or a nail. It will never come loose!

10) Now you can tie a bowline! Thank yor mouse: set a plate of cheese next to his hole tonight.

"The bowline is sometimes called the king of knots, and is the most useful way to form a loop in the end of a rope. It never slips or jams; and after severe tension has been applied to it, a simple push of the finger will loosen it enough to untie."
Encyclopedia of KNOTS and Fancy Rope Work, Cornell Maritime Press.

Left thumb and forefinger hold the bottom of the mouse hole, while the mouse waits behind the broom handle.

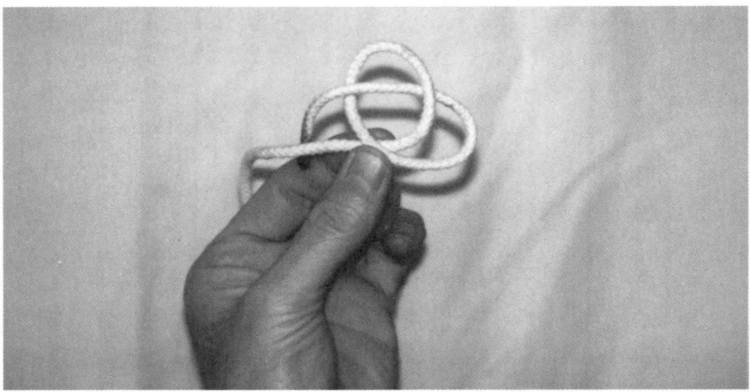

The mouse is ready to jump through mouse hole. Note the hand switch: right thumb and forefinger clamp the bottom of the mouse hole; left thumb and forefinger hold anxious mouse.

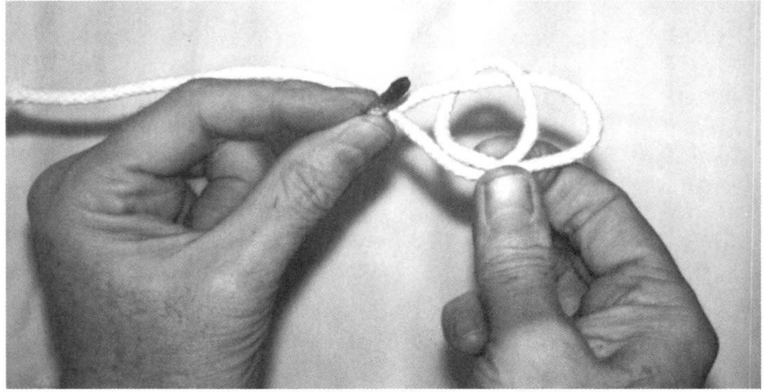

HOW TO READ MINDS

1) Say to a friend, "I can read your mind." The friend will answer, "No way. Go ahead, prove it." Then you prove it, as follows:

2) Ask your pal to think of a number between 1 and 9. She'll nod. Then you say, "Okay, multiply the number by 9."

3) Say, "If it's a two-digit number, add the two digits together, but don't tell me. Do it in your mind." Now tell her to substract the number 5.

4) Next step: Ask your doubting dodo to correspond the number with a letter, e.g., 1 is A, 2 is B, 3 is C, and so on. Now here comes the really fun part. Say, "Think of a country that begins with that letter." Pause. "Think of an animal that begins with the last letter in the country name." Pause. "Finally, think of a fruit that begins with the last letter in the animal's name."

5) Now for the clincher. Say, "I know what you're thinking. I can read your mind. You're in Denmark with a Kangaroo eating an Orange." Your stupified friend will fall on the floor. So what's the trick?

6) Here's another one, even better. Say, "I know your favorite number and the loose change in your pocket." "Impossible," they'll say.

7) "Oh, yeah, I'll prove it to you. Think of your favorite number and multiply it by 2. Add 5. Then multiply that number by 50. Use a calculator, or paper and pencil if you have to."

8) "Count the loose change in your pocket, add it to the last number, multiply it by 4, then subtract 1000."

9) Ask your skeptical buddy to tell you the final number. Let's say it's 2188. Without telling him, divide 2188 by 400, which equals <u>547</u>. Tell him, "Your favorite number is <u>5</u>, the loose change in your pocket is <u>47</u> cents." "How did you know?!" "Easy," you say, "I'm a mindreader."

10) If your buddy challenges you, hit him with another. Say, "Think of a number, but don't tell me. Double it. Add 12. Add 5. Subtract 3. Now, divide what you've got by 2, and subtract the number you started with." Smile. "Your number, dear friend is 7." Smile again.

A young man enters a small carnival tent lured by a sign that reads: ***For $50 I'll teach you to be a mind reader.*** An old man inside greets him: "Ah, you must be here for the mind reading lesson," as he hands the young man a hose.
"What's this?" the young man asks.
The old man replies, "It's part of the lesson. Look in the end of the hose and tell me what you see."
The young man peers inside the hose and says, "I see only darkness." Just then the old man turns on the tap, and the hose shoots water in the youngster's face.
"I knew you'd do something like that," the young man shouts.
"That'll be $50," said the old man.

Special Bonus Mindreading Trick

Say to your chum, "I know the number of brothers, sisters and grandparents you have, AND I CAN PROVE IT!"

Say, "Listen closely. Take the number of brothers you have, multiply by 2, add 3, times 5. Now, add your sisters to that number, multiply by 10. Lastly, add your grandparents, then add 125. Tell me the number."

You subtract 275 from the number your chum gives you (get, for example, 010), then say, "0 brothers, 1 sister, and 0 grandparents." Tell your stunned friend to breathe again, but don't reveal the secret.

HOW TO PULL PHONE PRANKS

1) With the advent of caller ID, e-mail and answering machines, the harmless telephone prank is no longer fashionable. It's time to resurrect this lost artform.

2) The classic joke that everyone should know goes as follows: Call a number at random, ask whoever answers, "Madam (or Sir), is your refrigerator running?" The answer, invariably, is, "Of course." You say, "Well, you better go catch it!"

3) Try these other jokes. Have fun!

4) At random, over several weeks, call the same number and ask, "Is Joe there?" If the party answers, "Who is this," just say, "I have a message for Joe," and hang up.

5) To avoid detection, don't call from home. Call from pay phones, ask your school pals to help you on this one, the more the merrier.

6) After several weeks and tons of phone calls, have a buddy ring up (preferably after midnight) and say, "This is Joe. Any messages for me?"

Here's another. Call a number, say, "This is the us station, Mr. (or Ms.) ______, we have a package r you down here. Will you pick it up?"

Most likely they'll say, "What kind of package?" ou say, "It's a crate of eggs, Sir (or Madam)."

"Eggs? Where are they from?" You say, hickens, stupid." Hang up.

0) Call a friend, ask "What do you have on tonight." hey'll say, "Oh, nothing." You say, "Cold, isn't it."

1) Call someone. "Hello, is this the City Dump?" hey'll answer: "No, this is the Jones residence." ay, "Well, I didn't miss by much, did I?"

2) Phone a Pizza parlor, ask, "Do you deliver?" Good, come quick! The pains are coming three inutes apart."

3) Remember, telephone pranks are fun, keep hem harmless. You don't yell "fire" in a crowded heater, and you don't do so in a telephone receiver ther.

On March 10, 1896, two days after the first intelligible communication by telephone, Alexander Graham Bell wrote in his laboratory notebook:

I shouted into [the mouthpiece] the following sentence: "Mr. Watson—Come here—I want to see you." To my delight he came and declared he heard what I said.

Bell's summons to Watson is one of history's most famous utterances, of that there is no doubt. But the notion that he did so because he had just spilled acid on his clothes is a fiction—indeed, if true, it would be the world's first telephone prank. Think about it. What would you say after spilling sulphuric acid on your pants? "Mr. Watson—Come here?" No way! You'd say something like, "AagghhhHH! This stuff burns! It's eating my leg. Watson, bring a bucket of water, fast."

HOW TO PERFORM A MAGIC CARD TRICK

1) Find the <u>six</u> and <u>nine</u> of diamonds in a standard deck of cards.

2) Place the <u>six</u> of diamonds on the bottom of the deck, <u>nine</u> of diamonds on the top.

3) Seat yourself at a table. Ask a friend to sit across the table from you, ask "Want to see a magic card trick?" The answer will, of course, be "Yes."

4) Flip the <u>nine</u> of diamonds on the table. (Don't let your friend see that it came from the top of the deck).

5) Spread the deck using both hands. Tilt the fanned deck up slightly—cards face out—to show your chum it's an ordinary—and not a trick—deck. Keep <u>six</u> of diamonds covered with left hand.

6) Say, "Go ahead, stick your card anywhere in the deck." Call the card a "card," not <u>nine</u> of diamonds.

') Fold the deck, place it on the table and square it ıp.

8) Shuffle the deck. Do an up-and-down shake huffle, then a flip shuffle. Make sure the six of liamonds stays on the bottom of the deck and away rom the watchful, prying eyes of your pal.

9) Shuffle the deck three more times. Tip. Distract our friend with chatter patter: "Seen this trick"? Ever see a magician in person before? On TV" Keep it up. Say anything, cloud your friend's mind.

10) Place deck on table, say, "To see your card tap he deck 3 times."

11) Pick up the deck, slap the deck against your open left hand 3 times, mumble, "abra ca dabra," and with a flourish, flip the six of diamonds from the bottom of the deck on the table. Your friend will confuse the six of diamond with "his" card, the nine of diamonds.

13) Your friend's mouth will open: "How'd you do hat." Never reveal the secret switcheroo. Say, "It's nagic." Try the six and nine of hearts instead of the six and nine of diamonds. Both work.

How many card phrases do you know?

- Stacked deck
- House of cards
- Show one's hand
- Know when to hold 'em, when to fold 'em
- What a card!
- Fast shuffle
- Not one's strong suit
- Holding your cards close to your vest
- Joker's wild
- Play one's cards right
- Put your cards on the table
- Double-dealing
- Not playing with a full deck
- One-eyed Jacks
- Jack's are wild
- Down and dirty
- Poker face
- Ace in the hole
- Read 'em and weep
- Card shark
- Inside straight
- Full House
- Royal Flush
- Blackjack
- Go fish
- Rummy
- Ante Up
- Make the pot right
- The Black Queen

HOW TO ADMINISTER THE DUMB TEST

1) Challenge a friend: "So you think you're smart, huh?! Let's see if you can pass the dumb test!"

2) Ask your friend to focus on the house (cover diagram left). Then tell the following tale.

3) "Inside the one-story house lives a crazy woman who has painted the ceiling, the floor, and the walls black. She's even painted the curtains, the furniture, and the windows black. So, smart person, what color did she paint the stairs?"

4) Your supposed smart friend will say, "Umm, well... of course, black."

5) You respond, "There are no stairs. It's a one-story house. Ha! Ha!"

6) "Okay, dumb one, let's move on, look at the diagram again, at the top."

7) Ask, "Which tree has the most leaves?"

8) Your friend will answer, "Ha! I got you, the middle one."

9) "No dummy, pine trees don't have leaves." Laugh, move on, hand your pal a pen, say, "Circle the largest X."

10) The dummy will circle the largest X on the right. Wrong! Take back the pen and circle the game X (the X separating the black house from the trees from the X's from The Dumb Test.) Say, "Oh, what a dummy dope-dope."

11) Now say, "Okay, buddy, one last chance to prove you have an ounce of intelligence." Hand him the pen. Tell him to, "Circle the dumb test."

12) After your friend circles The Dumb Test at the bottom, take back the pen, and draw a circle around the previous circle you drew. Say, "the Dumb Test is now nested with the house, the tree and the X's. Pay attention!"

13) Comfort your friend. No one likes to know they're stupid.

Cheer up, dimwits. There are people dumber than you, as the following student answers to high school and college test questions attest:

• H2O is hot water, and CO2 is cold water.
• When you smell an odorless gas, it is probably carbon monoxide.
• Dew is formed on leaves when the sun shines down on them and makes them perspire.
• Mushrooms always grow in damp places and so they look like umbrellas.
• A fossil is an extinct animal. The older it is, the more extinct it is.
• Magnet: Something you find crawling all over a dead cat.
• Momentum: What you give a person when they are going away.
• To keep milk from turning sour: Keep it in the cow.
• Blood flows down one leg and up the other.
• To remove dust from the eye, pull the eye down over the nose.
• The tides are a fight between the earth and the moon. All water tends toward the moon, because there is no water on the moon, and nature abhors a vacuum. I forget where the sun joins in this fight.
• A super saturated solution is one that holds more than it can hold.

www.stanford.edu/group/resed/wilb...onada/rinc9798/forwards/test-answers.htm

HOW TO DELIVER WHATSA JOKES

1) Whatsa jokes are set-up jokes. You feed a pal a line, he responds, then you pounce. Example: **The Set-up**. "Did you see the henway?" **The Whatsa**. What's a henway?" **The Pounce**. "About 3-4 pounds." You get the routine.

2) Try this. **The Set-up**: "Let's go by the trainway." **The Whatsa**: "What's a trainway?" **The Pounce**. "About 5 tons."

3) Try treeway, mooseway, cheeseway, wormway, wagonway. Have fun!

4) If someone asks you, "What do you want be when you grow up?" Answer, "A Monback." They'll ask, of course, "What's a Monback?" **Pounce**: "A guy who stands at a loading dock, in back of a truck, waving his hands, "'Mon back, mon back'." This works after you've grown up, too, when someone asks, "What do you do?" Say, "I'm a Monback."

5) People all the time inquire, "What's a matter?" You respond, "The matter is the one who takes the rags and straw and weaves it into a floor mat, or a car mat—it doesn't matter."

) Hey, turn your tired Knock-Knock jokes into /hatsa jokes. Example: "Is that an auga you're 'earing?" "What's an auga?" **Pounce**. "Ah, go ımp in the lake."

) Instead of auga, say, "hannah." **Pounce**: "Hannah ver your money, this is a stick up!" Say, "takoma." **ounce**: "Takoma here and I'll tweak your nose." r say, "Jose." **Pounce**: "Jose can you see?"

) Remember to vary your setup line. "Bring some swald when you come over." "Whatsa Oswald" Ɔs-wald my bubblegum, bring more."

) Say, "Bring my cowfor." "What's a cowfor?" Milk." The "——for" type setups are endless: axefor?" "Chopping trees." "kissfor?" "Love."

0) Another variation: At a diner booth, with your uddies, the waiter comes over, says, "What will you ave?" You answer, "A go-away salad." "What's a go-way salad? **Pounce**. "Lettuce alone."

1) Make up your own Whatsa jokes. Record them n a notebook so you won't forget them. Use them vhen things turn serious.

So you wanna know whatsa funny?

Worst analogies ever written in a high school essay contest:

* The little boat gently drifted across the pond exactly the way a bowling ball wouldn't.

* McBride fell 12 stories, hitting the pavement like a Hefty Bag filled with vegetable soup.

* Her hair glistened in the rain like nose hair after a sneeze.

* Her eyes were like two brown circles with big black dots in the center.

* Her vocabulary was as bad as, like, whatever.

* The hailstones leaped from the pavement, just like maggots when you fry them in hot grease.

* The politician was gone but unnoticed, like the period after the Dr. on a Dr Pepper can.

* John and Mary had never met. They were like two hummingbirds who had also never met.

* His thoughts tumbled in his head, making and breaking alliances like underpants in a dryer without Cling Free.

HOW TO TELL GIRLS FROM BOYS

1) You've probably noticed, girls are different than boys. But, sometimes, you can't always tell. Here are four sure fire tests.

2) Ask the subject (matters not whether you think it's a boy or a girl), "Please look at the ceiling."

3) The subject will either tilt its head backward (sometimes its entire upper torso), eyes flush with the ceiling, or keep its head erect and rotate its eyeballs upward, straining the eyesockets. If the former: It's a girl! Unlike boys, girls are more trusting, less wary, willing to take their eyes off their inquisitor.

4) Next. Say to subject, "Show me your fingernails."

5) If subject extends the hand and fingers straight out, palm down, nails in your face, then it's a boy. On the other hand (no pun intended), if subject pushes hand forward, fingers curled, nails up, well, what else, it's a girl.

6) True, girls are more trusting and likely to thrust their hand out, but in this instance, girls want to check out their nails (are the cuticles perfectly crescent?) as much as show them. Boys, of course, could care less what their fingernails look like.

) Next query: Without actually doing it, emonstrate how you would take your sweater off?

) A boy will tear his sweater off. Grasping the fabric round the neck and shoulders—sometimes in the ont, sometimes in back—one hand on either side nd yank. And squirm, as if that would help. Picture oudini escaping from a straightjacket.

) With girls, it's a ballet gesture. Hands grasping ie sweater at the bottom, arms crisscrossing at the aist, the arms rise up until the arms are fully xtended overhead, then a flick of the wrist, and the weater floats to the floor. Ahh, pure grace!

0) Now ask, show me how you would hold a baby oll? A pretend baby doll.

1) Girls will either cradle the doll in their arms ke Madonna and child or place the doll over their ft shoulder (their heart) in the burbing mode.

2) Boys, on the other hand, who have been ocialized to shy away from dolls, will embarrasingly old the pretend doll in one hand, like dragging a aggedy Andy doll, or in two hands in front of their ody as if handing you a dog taken from its bath.

3) There are other ways to tell boys from girls, but iey are not as reliable as the above questions. Use iem wisely and you will never be fooled.

"Thank heaven for little girls
For little girls get bigger every day
Thank heaven for little girls
They grow up in the most delightful way
Those little eyes so helpless and appealing
One day will flash and send you crashing through the ceiling
Thank heaven for little girls
Thank heaven for them all
No matter where, no matter who
Without them what would little boys do?"

Lyrics by Alan Jay Lerner, music by Frederick Lowe, from the stageplay and movie Gigi. © 1957 by Chappell & Co., Inc. Sung in the movie by Maurice Chevalier. Also starring Leslie Caron.

The How-To Cowboy demonstrating that he is indeed a cowboy. Note how he shows you his fingernails, while struggling to take off his sweater.

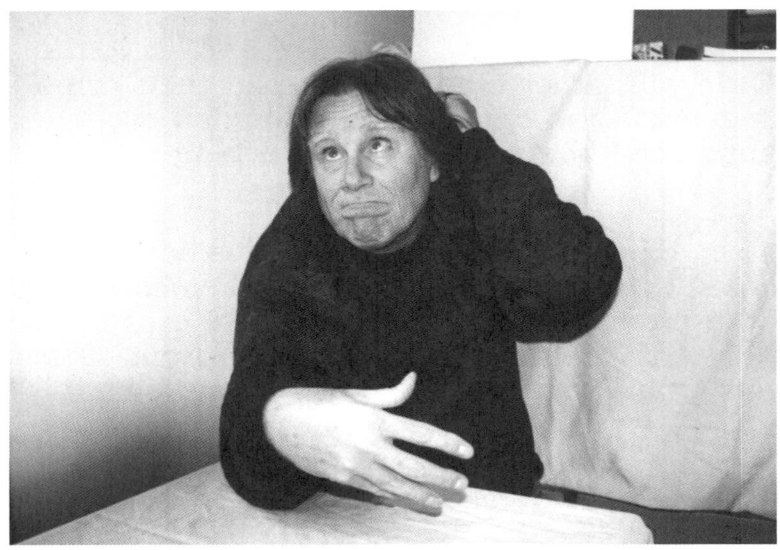

HOW TO SUMMON AN ANGEL

1) Say to a doubting person, "I can summon an angel." Before they pooh pooh your claim say, "I can prove it to you. Just follow my instructions."

2) Fist your hands, raise them to your face (either side of your nose), and point your index fingers at your eyes. Tell the skeptic to look into your eyes as you point your index fingers at your eyes and then thiers. Be sure to use both index fingers.

3) Tell the person that you are going to count to 3, pointing from your eyes to theirs at each count.

4) Next you say, "On the count of 3, I want you to close your eyelids, and keep them closed. I will then touch them briefly, at which time you will feel the presence of a heavenly angel." Here, elaborate a little, tell the person that people respond differently in the presence of an angel, some feel a brief chill, others a tug at their pant leg, still others a slight breeze. Lay it on thick.

5) Begin: index fingers pointing from your eyes to theirs. On 3, touch their closed eyelids <u>not</u> with your left and right index fingers but with your right index and middle fingers. Hold them there for a second while your free left hand gently swipes their shoulder, or hair. Quickly bring your left hand to the set position, index fingers pointing to their now open eyes. Nod as they gasp, "I felt an angel."

6) To really bamfoozle your friends, ready the Angel-Rings-The-Bell trick as follows.

7) Obtain a bouncing spider. You know, one of those hairy Tarantula-looking things that jump when you squeeze a little rubber ball. Underneath the spider you'll find a bellows (looks like a jelly roll until you squeeze the ball, and then it flattens out). Remove the bellows keeping the connecting air tube and the rubber ball intact.

8) Find a a little bell. Then find a decorative object like a Christmas tree, a candleabra, or an artsy doo-dad that you can hang the little bell on. Place your chosen object on a table or mantle. Place the bellows under the object. Run a test: squeeze the ball to make the the object jiggle so the bell will ring.

10) Now the hard part. You've got to hide the bellows and the connecting tube from view. Cover it up, or slip it through a crack, disguise it somehow.

11) Now the fun part. Invite a doubting person into your lair. Tell them, "I have the power to summon an angel." They'll say, "Yeah, sure." You answer, "Okay, doubtful one, I'll summon up an angel for you, but you won't see it, you'll just feel it, and that little bell over there on the Christmas tree will ring." Then, as you move into position, grasp the out-of sight rubber ball, say, "I summon an angel ... NOW!." Pause, then squeeze, and watch the doubters face drop in awe. "Tinkle. Tinkle."

Zuzu Bailey

(Christmas bell tinkles)
"Look, Daddy." (Pause) "Teacher says everytime a bell rings an angel gets his wings."

George Bailey

"That's right, that's right." (Looks heavenward, winks) "Way to go, Clarence."

It's A Wonderful Life (1946)
Directed by Frank Capra

HOW TO FOOL MOTHER NATURE

1) Want to fool Mother Nature? Wow your friends with a stunning floral centerpiece? A Boffo Bouquet? Then perk up those drab, store-bought *natural* flowers with food dye.

2) Start with white carnations and McCormicks® red, yellow, green and blue food dyes. Place a single carnation with a 6-7 inch stem in each of four cups, add dye and water in equal proportion, red dye in one, yellow in another, ditto green and blue.

3) In ten short hours, you will begin to see your white carnations take on a different hue, but for best results let them sit overnight and, in the morning, awake to four colorific flowers: red, yellow, green and blue.

4) Next, make your own colors. Mix yellow and red (orange), red and blue (purple), green and yellow (puce?), red and green (brown). Make your own shades by varying the amount of dye in the water.

5) Celebrate the holidays in style: green carnations for St. Patrick's Day; red, white and blue for the Fourth of July; yellow to welcome Spring any time of the year; orange carnations for Halloween; brown for Earth Day; red and green for Christmas; red for Valentines Day; and pink for the birth of a baby girl!

6) And, if you really want to fool Mother Nature, make a rainbow flower! Let the carnation sit in red dye for several hours, watch closely. Then, after several petals have turned red, slip the stem in green dye, then blue, the yellow. Oh my! Dazzling!

7) When your friends ask, "What's happening?" Tell them, "It's osmosis, don't you know." Then you explain: "Osmosis is the tendency of a fluid to pass through a semipermeable membrane into a solution where its concentration is lower, thus equalizing the conditions on either side of the membrane." That'll shut them up.

8) Create. Make your own ferns with leafy celery stalks and green dye.

9) Use other flowers, too. How about pink daisies? Green dye turns them mauve. Red dye gives them a crimson tinge. The posiblities are endleeesssssssss! Astors, too. And mums: football mums, spider mums.

10) In spring, tinge the fringe of your yellow daffodils and silky white jonquils green or red. In summer ... it's not nice to fool Mother Nature, so be careful, don't go too far, she could take revenge. (Hint: Who contols floods, tornados and hurricanes?)

In a series of successful commercials for Chiffon Margarine (1971-79), actress Dena Dietrich starred as Mother Nature who sampled the buttery taste of Chiffon Margerine. When she realized that Chiffon Margarine was not butter and that she had been tricked, she let lightning fly and earthquakes rumble to express her anger. Her trademark catchphrase was, **"It's not nice to fool Mother Nature!"**

A bouquet of flowers to dye for. Too bad you can't see them in color, but you get the idea.

HOW TO TONGUE-TIE A CHERRY STEM

1) Pick a cherry with a stem at least 2" long. Wash it. Wash your hands. Remove stem from fruit. Eat cherry, spit our seed. Note the end of the stem recently attached to the fruit: the knob end.

2) Slightly bend the cherry stem in half and stick it in your mouth. Swoosh it around. Get used to the idea that you've got a stem in your mouth.

3) Using tongue, cross the stem ends to form a fish—the knob to the front (teethside), the other end to the back (throatside).

4) Slide the tongue between the tail fins, slip tip of tongue underneath the knob and, ever so gently, work the knob over the bottom stem and through the body of the fish. Use the teeth to clamp down on the knob. Hold steady. Reach inside mouth, pull free stem end, and tighten the knot. Remove from mouth and display your stunning accomplishment to your astonished friends.

5) Now that you've tongue-tied a cherry stem knot in—shall we say—a rudimentary fashion, you are ready to perfect your talent and really wow your pals. First, don't bend the stem before you put it your mouth, do so in your mouth. Second, work on the end game, pull the cherry stem from your mouth with the knot tied in the middle, not near the end. This improvement will solicit even louder "Ooohs" and "Ahhhs." The key to centering the knot in the stem is to pull the knot back with the tip of your tongue while holding the knob end place with teeth.

6) The above instructions should be viewed as guidelines, not as hard and fast rules etched in cherry wood. As in most games of life, when all else fails, don't punt, improvise, find your own way. For example, some people say they can use either end of the cherry stem to "thread the fish," the decision usually made being made once the stem is resting comfortably in the mouth. And to others it matters not which end overlaps the other when forming the "fish."

7) If at first you don't succeed, remember how long it took you to tie your own shoes. Imagine trying to tie them with just one hand! How do you get to Carnegie Hall? Patience. Patience. Patience.

8) Caveat: A small percentage of people are hampered with an inflexible, rigid tongue. If you suspect you suffer from this malady, and daily exercize and proper diet have not improved the situation, see your physician. Therapy is usually prescribed. Corrective surgery is rarely used, and only then as a last resort. Tongue transplants are still in the research stage.

A lost soul is in line at the Pearly Gates. St. Peter asks, "How did you die?"
"Well, my friend and I were lost. So we stopped at a farmhouse and asked to stay the night. The farmer said, 'Only on one condition: go out in my field and pick a fruit — one with a stem — that you can put in your mouth, and hightail it back here.' I did as he told me, and when I returned he raised a shotgun and said, 'Put the cherry in your mouth, swallow the fruit, and then tie the stem in a knot with your tongue, and you'll live. And if you laugh, I'll shoot you dead.'
I swallowed the cherry and promptly tied a knot in the cherry stem with my tongue."
Puzzled, St. Peter asks, "Then why are you here?"
"I saw my friend coming up the walkway with a watermelon."

ANOTHER BOOK BY EDWARD ALLAN FAINE

A Chapter-Picture Book For Kids 4 - 8

'Here's an interesting idea — a chapter book for the younger set. The ɔook contains three separate stories — yarns, if you will — about a six-/ear old West Virginian named Ned and his rural lifestyle in the 1950s. The stories are divided into small, easy to read chapters and are what 'ou might call "wholoesome" — an antidote to current tendencies."

Elaine Gant, Los Angeles Family, "America's Largest Regional Family Magazine"

To order an autographed copy: send $10 (includes $1 S&H to: M Press, PO Box 5346, Takoma Park, MD 20913 and include nscription: "To Max, who loves stories."
nfo:efaine@yahoo.com 301-587-1202 Also available on Amazon.com

ANOTHER BOOK BY EDWARD ALLAN FAINE

A Story Book For Kids 10 - 13

"The most intriguing thing about this small paperback is that it remind one of William J. Bennett's book *The Book of Virtues—A Treasury* *Great Moral Stories*. Bennett's book is more than 800 pages; while *Ne Ventures* barely makes 64. But the same themes discussed by Benne run through the story topics in this book for they are used to describe way of life for a group of teens that would be difficult today anywhe in the United States. This book would be best viewed as a collection short, rather interesting fairy tales that could be classified as fictio

Martina B. Talafaro, Library Consultant, Silver Spring, Marylan

order an autographed copy: send $7 (includes $1 S&H to: ress, PO Box 5346, Takoma Park, MD 20913 and include ription: "To June, who loves reading." Info: efaine@yahoo.com 1-587-1202. Also available on Amazon.com.

ANOTHER BOOK BY EDWARD ALLAN FAINE
A Picture Book For Kids 2 – 6

this book, author Faine and Illustrator Waites lay the groundwork for ɔur child's first understanding of the major environmental challenge of ır time. Told in a straightforward and delightful way, the story of young dan's coming to grips with Global Warming – some of its causes, nsequences and what to do about it – is sure to hold your child's tention. Simple, easy to understand language is used throughout and, in ldition, avoids the use of next-level terminology such as greenhouse ıses and carbon dioxide. The book concludes with things kids can do to ılp Aidan save the world from Global Warming.

der this book individually, or in bulk at reduced price from:
Press P.O. Box 5346 Takoma Park, MD 20913
ntact: 301-587-1202 or efaine@yahoo.com

Edward Allan Faine is the author of ten children's books for ages 0-12. See them at:

www.google.com/profiles/edwardallanfaine

Mr. Faine (aka the How-To Cowboy) is an interactive children's entertainer who performs at daycares, schools, libraries, stores, markets and festivals. For the younger set he offers a "Show and Tell" of his picture books, and for kids 7 - 12 his How-To Cowboy routines: hand trumpet playing, neat knot tying, tongue/acorn whistling and Donald Duck/Darth Vader talking.

In addition, for the wider 1 -12 age range, Mr. Faine offers his How-To Cowboy JokeFest "Tell A Joke" "Get A Book." After stepping up to the joke mic and telling a joke (or for the younger ones, making an animal sound), the jokester receives a book of their choice authored by Mr Faine, signed and inscribed.

To view a typical How-To Cowboy JokeFest, type "Knock-knocks" into the search bar at:

www.washingtonpost.com

To read the accompanying article, type in "Kid comics"

And for those who love jokes, which means everyone, follow weeklyfrogjokes at:

www.twitter.com

Contact Mr. Faine at:

301-587-1202 efaine@yahoo.com